# Annabella's Crown

## Jeanne Dennis
### &
## Christine St. Jacques

ELK LAKE PUBLISHING INC

PUBLISHING THE POSITIVE
Plymouth, Massachusetts

Cover and Interior Design: Jeanne Dennis, Derinda Babcock
Editor(s): Derinda Babcock, Deb Haggerty
Illustrations: Jeanne Dennis

PUBLISHED BY: Elk Lake Publishing, Inc., 35 Dogwood Dr., Plymouth, MA 02360, 2020

_____

Library Cataloging Data
Names: Dennis, Jeanne and St. Jacques, Christine (Jeanne Dennis & Christine St. Jacques)
*Annabella's Crown* / Jeanne Dennis and Christine St. Jacques
40 p. 28 cm × 21.6 cm (8.5 in × 11 in.)
Identifiers: ISBN-13: 978-1-64949-320-0 (paperback) | 978-1-64949-321-7 (trade hardcover) | 978-1-64949-322-4 (trade paperback) | 978-1-64949-323-1 (e-book)
Key Words: Children's Royalty Books; Children's Christian Fantasy and Magic; Children's Siblings; Children's Values; Children's Cats Book; Christian Values & Virtues; Children's Folk Tales and Myths
Library of Congress Control Number: 2021944495 Fiction

# Dedication

Jeanne: For my co-author, the best daughter in the world, and for my illustration models: Grace, Amy, Cara, Noah, Noah, Mary, Francesca, Meadow, Steve, Emma, Lucy, John Mark, Grant, and of course, the cats.

Christine: For my dad and mom, who taught me what it means to be a daughter of the true King.

Once in a faraway kingdom, in a seashell-covered castle by the sea, lived Princess Annabella. She had a voice like springtime, a smile like sunshine, and stubbornness like a locked gate—which is why she almost missed her greatest treasure.

Annabella was the youngest of the king's children. She lived in the castle with her father, two sisters, two brothers, maids, cooks, butlers, gardeners, ladies in waiting, and me. I'm Leopold, the royal cat, at your service.

One morning, while the bullfrogs in the moat slept and the dew still shone on the grass, the king invited his daughters to join him in the rose garden. "Come, Belinda, Christina, and Annabella. I have something special to give you."

Sleepy-eyed Annabella followed slowly, using me as a pillow. I struggled free and found a dry spot to enjoy the fragrant blossoms.

The king's eyes gleamed as he spoke. "I've called you here to give you each a gift. Remember, things are not always as they appear. Sometimes they are ever so much more."

Christina tilted her head and eyed him curiously. "If things are not what they appear, then how shall we discover their worth?"

"You will find out in time." He handed each of his daughters a golden box.

Annabella threw open the lid. "Jewels! Thank you."

Christina and Belinda grinned. "Yes, thank you, Father."

"I'm glad you like your gifts. But remember—treasures fade in truth's light. Use your jewels wisely to find greater treasure." He smiled and left.

"Use them wisely?" Belinda stared at her gift.

Christina clapped her hands. "We have a mystery to solve!"

Annabella held a sapphire up to the sunlight. "I don't like mysteries. I like jewels." Suddenly, she gasped. "The sapphire's gone!"

"Did you drop it?" Christina searched the ground with her, but the gem had disappeared.

Annabella shouted over her shoulder as she hurried back to the castle. "I'm going to have a necklace made before I lose any more."

Christina stood up. "I think Father would like me to share these gems with the poor people of the village. I'll throw them from my coach and watch their happy faces."

That's what she said, but I know how much she enjoys hearing villagers shout, "Long live Princess Christina."

"I'm going to change clothes and ride to the village."

After Christina left, I climbed onto Belinda's lap, kneaded my paws on her velvet skirt, and settled into its folds.

"Oh, Leopold, I'm not clever like Christina or talented like Annabella. How can I use Father's gift wisely?"

She looked inside the jewel box again. "I know. I'll sell the jewels and buy him a gift."

I purred and stretched, accidentally knocking a few gems from the box. They faded away. *How strange. Time to search for answers.*

After a farewell meow, I scampered up the tower stairs to the princesses' chambers.

Annabella had arranged her jewels in a necklace shape. I hopped on the table.

"Leopold, be careful! You knocked some on the floor."

*Why do people always blame the cat? I didn't touch anything.* The jewels had simply vanished, just like Belinda's.

"I'll put my jewels in a safe place before I lose any more of them."

Annabella laid the box in a trunk. "I've had enough mystery for today." She skipped out of the room.

3

I rode with Christina to the village. While she tossed jewels to people in ragged clothes, I sat on the velvet seat of her carriage.

The villagers shouted, "Long live Princess Christina," as she had hoped.

Suddenly, the cheers turned to jeers. I looked back. "A mean trick," they shouted, now with empty hands.

Christina stared at the jewels in her box as we headed back to the castle.

That evening I rested on the windowsill of the dressing room while the princesses prepared for bed.

Annabella rushed in. "They're gone! My jewels are gone." She held an empty box.

Belinda and Christina checked their boxes. Empty.

Belinda fingered the golden lid. "I tried to sell my jewels to the royal jewelers to buy Father a present. But the gems kept disappearing."

Christina laid her box on a table. "Father said treasures fade in truth's light. I wonder what he meant."

"And what treasure is greater than jewels?"

Annabella yawned. "We can't do anything with disappearing jewels. You two can solve Father's mystery. I'm going to bed."

Annabella and I settled into satin covers.

She turned her head. "Listen, Leopold. Over and over, the sea races to the shore saying, 'Jewels, jewels, jewels,' with its breathy voice."

I yawned and put my head on my paws. To me, the sea whispered, "Sleep, sleep, sleep."

The next morning, I awoke to Christina's excited voice. "The boxes are full again, Belinda! How mysterious. Maybe we can discover more about them at breakfast. Let's hurry!"

Their gowns rustled as their footsteps faded down the hall.

I decided to follow them. As I hopped to the floor, Annabella turned over. A pillow fell off the bed on top of me. I jumped, carefully sniffed the pillow, and ran after the others to join the family for breakfast.

Belinda and Christina talked with their father as they finished their crêpes. I ate fish from my silver bowl. Then I groomed my sleek coat as I listened to the family's conversation.

Christina laid down her fork. "Father, you say the ancient writings contain wisdom. Will they explain the secret of the jewels?"

His eyes twinkled.

Christina jumped up and kissed his cheek. "I knew it. You have given us a mystery to solve."

She hurried toward the royal library. I licked up the last of my fish and bounded after her.

The library door creaked and dust floated in light streams from the stained-glass windows. We climbed to the upper floor, where many of the scrolls were kept. I relaxed as Christina read. Her open treasure box lay beside her.

"Do not become tired of doing good. In time you will have your reward." She sighed. "The villagers' clothes looked worn, and their children looked hungry. I'm sure I can help them."

A pink tourmaline flashed like fire and vanished. Christina's eyes sparkled. "Is doing good the secret of the jewels? Or reading the ancient writings?"

After a nap, I joined Belinda and the king in the throne room. Each day, people came asking for help or for pardon for things they had done wrong. Belinda held her jewel box as we listened to her father's judgments.

One young boy had been arrested for stealing a pig. He stole the animal because his widowed mother and young sisters were hungry. The king pardoned the boy and gave him a job. Part of the money he earned would pay for the pig.

"When you need help, ask me," the king told the boy.

Belinda paid close attention to her father's words. She didn't notice the lights shooting from her treasure box, but I did. I had to use all of my willpower not to bat at them. A royal cat must exercise control, especially before the king's subjects.

After everyone left, Belinda sat beside the king.

"Father, you show so much wisdom and kindness. No wonder your subjects love you."

He smiled. "Serving them brings me joy."

"*Serving* them? But you're the king."

"A good king serves his people."

Belinda laid down her jewel box. "Father, will you teach me to be like you?"

He looked at her lovingly. "Yes, my child. Stay with me."

A rainbow of light shot from Belinda's box. I pounced on the beam.

The king grinned and winked at me. I flitted my tail and blinked back as Annabella burst into the room.

"Father, why didn't I get breakfast? The table is set for lunch."

The king opened his arms to Annabella. "Where have you been this morning? I've missed you."

Annabella hugged him. "Father, you haven't answered my question."

"You know we give extra food to the poor."

"I forgot. And today my jewel box is only half full. Why?"

"Your box was full this morning," said Belinda. "I looked."

The king touched Annabella's cheek. "Act wisely, and you'll have full treasure and breakfast too. Come sing for me with your lute."

Annabella had the most beautiful voice in the kingdom. She knew how much her father loved to hear her sing.

"I'm too hungry," she said, and left.

Belinda stood up and touched the king's shoulder. "I don't have a pretty voice like Annabella's, but I'll sing for you, Father."

The king wrapped his arm around her. "Thank you, Belinda. Your voice is just as beautiful to me."

A yellow topaz from Belinda's box lit her face as she picked up the lute to sing.

Before bed, the princesses found the boxes empty again.

As her sisters took off their crowns, Annabella shrieked. "Where did you get *those*?"

Belinda and Christina examined their golden crowns.

I hopped up to see for myself. Several tiny gems on each crown gleamed in the evening light. I marveled at red rubies, blue sapphires, green emeralds, purple amethysts, yellow topazes, pink tourmalines, and the most beautiful diamonds I'd ever seen.

Belinda gave her crown a puzzled look. "I wonder where they came from. I wore my crown all day."

"So did I," Christina said. "I was reading the ancient scrolls."

Annabella removed her crown, still plain gold. "I played all day."

Christina patted her shoulder. "When we solve Father's mystery, you'll have jewels on your crown too."

Annabella headed for her room. "I don't care."

But I knew she cared—far more than she would admit.

Belinda and Christina rose early the next day. Before they left, they looked in on Annabella. She was sound asleep.

Belinda shook her sister gently. "Wake up, sleepyhead."

Annabella sighed.

Christina leaned close to Annabella. "Annabella, Annabella, don't you want to eat this morning?"

Annabella shot up. "No one will take breakfast from me today."

Belinda and Christina grinned as they left the room.

Annabella put on her gown and brushed her hair. "Somehow, I'll discover the secret. I will have jewels on my crown by tonight."

After breakfast, Christina carefully placed her full box of jewels into the pocket hidden in the folds of her skirt. Then she gathered food from the larder. We took a wagonload to the village. There the princess scrubbed floors, cooked meals, and washed children's faces. She had shoes made for their bruised, muddy feet. Then she entertained the children with her stories.

I entertained them with my charm.

While busy serving the people, Christina forgot about her treasure box. But one toddler followed her, giggling each time lights glowed from Christina's pocket.

Annabella was still eating when we returned to the palace for a late lunch.

Christina told her about our morning with the villagers. "The people need so much help. Why don't you come with me this afternoon?"

"Have you discovered the secret of the jewels yet?"

"No, I forgot about them."

Annabella wiped her mouth with a napkin. "Then I can't go. I'm going to read the ancient scrolls and try to find the answer."

Christina cocked her head to the side and smiled in amusement. "I thought you didn't care about Father's mystery."

Annabella shrugged. "I do now." She skipped from the room.

I bounded after her. Afternoon sunbeams on the library's mahogany table make it the best spot in the castle for a nap.

I should have taken my time. Before we reached the library, Isaac, the minstrel, greeted Annabella.

"Good day, Princess. May I play your favorite song?"

Annabella never refused to hear the song about a princess captured by a dragon and rescued by a knight.

As Annabella hummed along and spun to the music, her laughter rippled through the corridor.

During one twirl, her crown flew off and hit my head. I yowled and jumped out of the way. The crown didn't hurt much, but it mussed my fur.

As Isaac came to the end of the ballad, Annabella sang along.

> "This bravest of knights scaled the dragon's scales
> To the cheering and waving of banners.
> He stood on its snout, looked it straight in the eye.
> Then he let out a sigh, calmly flicked off a fly,
> As the crowd heard him cry,
> 'Eating princesses? Shocking bad manners.'"

Annabella giggled.

Isaac bowed. "Shall I play the song again, Princess?"

"No, thank you. I have to find my father."

"He is in Knight's Hall. Your brothers and the other knights have chivalry training today."

"Thank you, Isaac. I will go find him."

*I thought we were headed for the library and my sunny spot.* I glared at her, stretched, and followed her anyway.

Annabella skipped towards Knight's Hall, humming.

Soon we heard her father's strong voice speaking to the knights. Annabella stopped a few feet from the hall's entrance. We listened as the king finished reviewing the qualities knights must display.

When the meeting ended, the knights, squires, and pages filed out the door. Among them were Annabella's brothers, Peter and Henry.

Henry smiled at Annabella as he passed. With dark hair, he stood strong and broad-shouldered, resembling their father.

Peter was younger than Henry and a few inches shorter. His eyes gleamed with mischief. Peter grinned at Annabella and gave her hair a playful tug. Annabella tried to mess up his perfectly combed mass of flax-colored hair, but he moved too quickly.

Her laughter echoed as she entered the hall.

The king came towards her. "There's my delightful girl."

"I had breakfast today."

*And a long lunch*, I wanted to add.

They hugged.

"Father, last night Belinda and Christina had jewels in their crowns. Why doesn't mine have jewels?"

"You must discover the reason for yourself."

"But how?"

The king stooped to her level. "Do you love me, Annabella?"

"Of course I do."

"Then sing for me." The king motioned to a lute in the corner.

"But you didn't answer my question."

"Are you sure? Let's take a walk together in the garden."

"No, thanks. I have a mystery to solve first."

Annabella headed for the library. As she pushed open the thick door, I sniffed odors of old wood and parchment. She rolled out a scroll on my favorite table.

I jumped up and lay on my back, soaking up the sun's rays.

"I'll read more than Christina did and get twice as many jewels on my crown."

I wiggled under Annabella's hand for a tummy rub.

Annabella sighed. "Leopold, I'd much rather play with you than read these dusty, old things."

I twisted to remind her to pet me.

Annabella brushed me softly and stared at the scroll. "Look! This part must be about the jewels." She slid me aside.

*How rude!*

"'Children obey your parents. Honor them, for this brings great reward.'"

Annabella sat back in her chair. "I was unkind to Father. He asked me to sing for him and walk with him, but I refused. I must go tell him I'm sorry."

I jumped down and meowed to encourage her, but the bell rang for tea.

"Food! I'll race you."

I had to scramble to protect my tail as Annabella charged out of the room.

Belinda and the king chatted during tea. Annabella said nothing. She pretended to pay attention to her food. But her eyes flashed when she sneaked glances at Belinda and their father.

Afterwards, their father invited both girls to walk around the duck pond with him. Belinda readily agreed, but Annabella refused. Belinda and the king left arm in arm.

Annabella fumed. "So Belinda has charmed Father with her sweetness and Christina with her kindness. I'll outdo them both."

Annabella darted outside, heading in the opposite direction from the pond.

She searched until she found the head gardener. "Good afternoon, Miles. I'll help with anything that won't get me dirty."

*Hmph. If humans had sandpapery tongues like mine, dirt wouldn't bother them.* I flopped into a bed of daisies.

Miles chuckled. "Well, Princess, I'm sure we can find a task for you. Thank you for coming to help."

Annabella spent the afternoon picking peaches. Then she served supper with the servants. She kept sighing until she got her father's attention. Each time he looked at her, she tried to smile sweetly, but her face wrinkled like a prune.

I rolled on the floor, laughing silently as only a cat can.

Later that night, Belinda's and Christina's crowns had new stones.

"I can't wait to see my jewels." Annabella removed her crown. She frowned. "Hmmm. Still plain gold."

Annabella told her sisters good night and quickly withdrew to her chamber. I followed, knowing she needed me. By the time she fell asleep, her ears, hair, and my fur were soaked with tears.

The next morning, Annabella woke before anyone else, even the servants. She picked fruit, scrubbed the larder floor, polished the throne, and helped with breakfast.

After she finished eating, the king asked Annabella to sing for him. She actually got angry and stomped out.

I growled at her and then jumped on the king's lap, hoping to ease his sadness with gentle purrs.

Christina soon came to fetch me for another outing. I was surprised to see Annabella waiting in the royal carriage.

Instead of singing for the king, Annabella spent the day with Christina, helping the poor villagers. I chased mice away from the food baskets.

Annabella told me she enjoyed serving, but she looked gloomy. I think her conscience gnawed at her.

I gnawed at a flea.

After supper, Annabella swept the great hall. I sat on a chair and stared at her. Someone had to get through to that silly princess.

"What's wrong with you?"

I had her.

"Leopold, don't you see? I have to show Father I'm better than my sisters. Besides, what do you care? You already have a jeweled collar."

*Yes, and I'm proud of my collar, which I wear only for special occasions.*

Annabella trudged upstairs. "A day like today deserves diamonds." Her hands trembled as she removed her crown. "What? Nothing! After all my work?"

She rushed downstairs to the throne room. Before we reached the door, we heard Belinda finish a song.

Annabella stopped abruptly. "What's she doing? Singing for Father is my job."

The king praised Belinda's singing and Christina's hard work.

Annabella huffed away. "I worked harder than Christina. And I have a prettier voice than Belinda, but *they* get the jewels *and* Father's attention. He keeps asking me to do more when he knows how busy I am."

She pretended to be asleep when her sisters came upstairs to go to bed.

In the middle of the night, Annabella's whisper woke me. "If I can't have jewels on my crown, neither can they."

Annabella crept into the parlor the princesses shared. I watched from behind the door. Her sisters' crowns sparkled in the moonlight. Annabella reached for them but pulled back. She shivered and rubbed the back of her neck. Then she glanced around as if hidden eyes (besides mine) peered at her through the darkness. Her eyes looked black and empty.

My skin quivered.

Annabella snatched both crowns, hurried back to her chamber, and shut the door.

*Smash!* Two crowns hit the floor. I scrambled under the bed. Over and over, Annabella threw the crowns until the jewels fell from their settings and faded away.

She gasped. "What have I done? Father will never forgive me."

Then she stomped her foot. "I don't care. It's not fair." She grabbed the crowns and dashed to the window.

I hissed a warning and leapt onto the windowsill too late to stop her. She tossed the crowns out into the night. Together we watched her sisters' once glorious crowns sink into the moat.

The next morning, Annabella held her stomach. Her face looked green. "How can I face them after what I did?"

When we entered the parlor, Annabella froze and my fur stood on end.

Belinda's and Christina's crowns rested on a pillow, as beautiful as before. Annabella's crown, which smelled gloriously of fish, sat beside them bent and covered with algae. I jumped up for a taste, but Annabella snatched her crown away.

She stormed back to her room and flopped on the bed, sobbing. "Why is this happening to me?"

Her sisters rushed in to see what had upset her.

Belinda rubbed Annabella's back. "Come to breakfast. You'll feel better after you eat something."

Annabella pulled away and threw her crown on the floor. "I'm not hungry."

Belinda and Christina stared at each other, shocked. They hurried out.

Soon the king knocked on the door. When Annabella didn't answer, he came in and set a tray of food beside her. "Would you like to talk?"

Annabella sobbed her reply. "You praised Belinda and Christina and gave them jewels on their crowns. You ... love ... them ... more than me."

The king's eyes filled with tears. "You know I love my children equally. Nothing could change my love for you." He tenderly brushed hair off her soaked face.

"But they have jewels on their crowns! My crown is a mess."

"I didn't give your crown to you that way. Your actions bring their own results."

"I did *more* work than they did. Don't I deserve jewels too?"

"Yes, you worked hard, but why?"

Annabella took shaky breaths between words. "I ... want ... jewels ... in my crown."

The king stroked her face. "What about love, Annabella?" He picked up her crown and placed it on the bed.

After he left, Annabella moved to the window seat. She stared out at the castle grounds and sobbed, choking on each breath.

I couldn't bear to hear a princess weeping, so I climbed up to comfort her. She held onto me for a long time.

Finally, she calmed down. "Oh, Leopold, I'm a terrible daughter. I refused to sing for my father or spend time with him. I didn't respect or obey him like the ancient writings said. And I was jealous of my sisters."

I looked up and gave a soft meow. A tear landed on my fur.

"Father still loves me, even though I thought only about myself."

Suddenly, she sat up straighter. "Treasures *do* fade in truth's light. The truth is I love Father more than jewels, crowns, or anything else."

I licked Annabella's hand and gave her my rumbliest purr.

That afternoon, Annabella wore her bent, dirty crown into the throne room. Everyone stared as she headed towards the line of subjects who had come to speak with her father.

When the king saw her, he immediately left the throne and wrapped her in his arms.

She knelt before him. "Father, I haven't been a good daughter. I'm so sorry. From now on, I want to please you. I will obey whatever you ask, because I love you. Please forgive me."

Annabella laid her crown at her father's feet as her body shook with sobs.

The king's face filled with tenderness. He lifted her chin and smiled. "Annabella, my beautiful daughter, you have learned the secret. Well done."

Annabella's father raised her to her feet. He picked up her crown, which now sparkled with jewels, and placed it on her head.

Annabella always says that was the moment she realized her real treasure, her true crown, was seeing the diamond-like sparkle of pleasure in her father's eyes.

"Sing for me, Annabella."

Annabella's singing filled the palace with joy like a fresh spring rain. And the glitter of Annabella's crown could not compare with the glow of love on her father's face.

I curled up in the king's lap and purred in perfect harmony.

# The End

If you know Jesus, place your picture on this page to remind you of your identity as a forever child of our heavenly King.

# Are You the Heavenly King's Child?

God, the Creator and King of the Universe, loves you so much he sent his only son, Jesus, to pay for everything you've ever done wrong. (Doing wrong is called sin.) You can't do anything to make God love you more. You can't do anything to make God love you less.

Just as Annabella's father loved her even when she acted ugly, Jesus loves you when you make mistakes. He died for you, even though he knew you would sin, and even though you had not yet loved him back. Then he rose from the dead, and you can have eternal life in heaven with him.

Remember when Annabella's father wrapped her in his arms? If you turn away from sin and accept God's gift of salvation, he will come into your heart and wrap you in his love. He will never leave you. You will be a loved child of the King forever and ever.

Have you given your life to Jesus? If not, now is a good time. If you are truly sorry for your sins and you want to live for God, tell him now. Give him your life and ask him to help you love and obey him every day.

Sometimes you will fail and not obey God perfectly. When you fail, ask him to forgive you and help you start again. You will soon discover the priceless jewels God has for you: love, joy, peace, and so many others. (You can find some of them in Galatians 5:22–23).

Living your life in love with Jesus brings the greatest treasures of all.

Learn about being a child of the heavenly King in the Bible. Read John 3:16–19; Ps. 103:17; Rom. 3:23, 5:8, 5:12, 6:23, 10:9–10, 10:13; Matt. 28:19–20; 1 John 1:9; and Eph. 1:3–14. Also visit https://jeannedennis.com/annabella for more information and fun *Annabella's Crown* activities.

# About Jeanne Dennis

Jeanne Dennis, coauthor and illustrator of *Annabella's Crown*, is the multi-award-winning author of over a dozen books. In 2011, she co-founded the online ministry Heritage of Truth to help families nurture lifelong confidence in biblical truth. A Colson Fellow and Centurion, Jeanne helps support parents and grandparents with resources that promote and explain the biblical worldview in ways children can understand. She and her husband serve actively in their local church. Jeanne's favorite pastimes include art, singing and writing music, teaching Sunday school, and enjoying God's creation with her family.

# About Christine St. Jacques

Christine St. Jacques, coauthor of *Annabella's Crown* and Jeanne's daughter, has over twenty years of experience working in creative arts. She has spent much of her time directing and teaching theatre, has performed in many plays and musicals, and has spent years choreographing the musicals she's directed. She started writing as a hobby in elementary school and has had several works published. In her spare time, Christine enjoys visiting the mountains and the beach with her husband and children. She also likes relaxing with her cats, who served as the models for Leopold.

Made in the USA
Columbia, SC
02 May 2022

59839061R00024